For Lily
R.C.

For Alice and Thomas
P.H.

First published in Great Britain in 1997
by WH Books Ltd
an imprint of Reed Children's Books
Michelin House, 81 Fulham Road, London SW3 6RB
and Auckland, Melbourne, Singapore and Toronto

ISBN 0 434 80033 3

Produced by Mandarin Offset Ltd
Printed and bound in China

Mouse Creeps

Peter Harris · illustrations by Reg Cartwright

HEINEMANN · LONDON

Dog sleeps.
Mouse creeps.

Cat sees.

Mouse flees.

Horse shies.
Churn flies.

Ducks wake.
Pigs escape.

Ducks fly.
Hunters spy.

Drums beat.

Armies meet.

Soldiers fear.
Battle near.

Drummer sighs.
Then surprise!

Acorns tumble.
General stumbles.

The other drops.
Fighting stops.

Soldiers roar.
End war.

Father at door.
Soldier no more.

Dog sleeps.
Mouse creeps.